8-10

D1007178

# Dora's Picnic

by Christine Ricci
illustrated by Susan Hall

SCHLEICHER CO. PUBLIC LIBRARY
BOX 611-201 S MAIN
PH 325-853-3767
ELDORADO, TEXAS 76936-0611

Ready-to-Read

Simon Spotlight/Nick Jr.

New York London Toronto Sydney Singapore

Based on the TV series *Dora the Explorer*® as seen on Nick Jr.®

SIMON SPOTLIGHT
An imprint of Simon & Schuster Children's Publishing Division
1230 Avenue of the Americas,
New York, New York 10020
Copyright © 2003 Viacom International Inc.
All rights reserved. NICKELODEON, NICK JR., *Dora the Explorer,*
and all related titles, logos, and characters are trademarks of Viacom International Inc.
All rights reserved, including the right of reproduction in whole or in part in any form.
READY-TO-READ, SIMON SPOTLIGHT, and colophon
are registered trademarks of Simon & Schuster.
Manufactured in the United States of America

6 8 10 9 7 5

Ricci, Christine.
Dora's picnic / by Christine Ricci.
p. cm.—(Ready-to-read. Level 1, Dora the explorer ; 1)
Summary: Dora and her animal friends all contribute something to bring to
a picnic at Play Park. Features rebuses.
ISBN 0-689-85238-X
1. Rebuses. [1. Picnicking—Fiction. 2. Animals—Fiction. 3. Parks—Fiction. 4. Rebuses.]
I. Title. II. Series.
PZ7.R355 Do 2003
[E]—dc21
2002004518

Hi! I am . We are
DORA
going to a picnic at Play
Park! Play Park has a ,
SLIDE
a , and .
SANDBOX
SWINGS

My **mami** is helping me make -and- sandwiches for the picnic.

PEANUT-BUTTER JELLY

BOOTS is my best friend.

He loves BANANAS!

BOOTS has a bunch of BANANAS for the picnic.

BENNY is riding his BICYCLE to
the picnic.

He is carrying  juice

APPLE

in his  .

BASKET

Here comes the  .

BIG RED CHICKEN

The  has a big  of

BIG RED CHICKEN

BAG

 for the picnic.

POPCORN

Yummy!

Look! has a bowl of

BABY BLUE BIRD

fruit in her .

WAGON

The fruit bowl has ,
BANANAS
, and .
APPLES
GRAPES

What did bring to
TICO
the picnic?

TICO brought BREAD.
The BREAD is filled with
BLUEBERRIES and NUTS!

ISA made CUPCAKES to share with everyone.

I like chocolate CUPCAKES with PINK icing. What kind do you like?

Look out for  .

SWIPER

He will try to swipe the food we brought.

SWIPER

is hiding behind

the  .
TREE

Say, "Swiper, no swiping!"

Yay! You stopped  !
SWIPER

We made it to Play Park!

This  is perfect for

TABLE

our picnic. But first we want to play!

likes to go down
TICO
the .
SLIDE

is making a
BABY BLUE BIRD
SAND CASTLE
in the .
SANDBOX

The  pushes 

BIG RED CHICKEN BOOTS

and  on the  .

ISA SWINGS

This is the best picnic!
We can all share the food.
What would **you** bring
to a picnic?